HOLD THIS!

Written by Carolyn Cory Scoppettone

Illustrations by Priscilla Alpaugh

Published by Islandport Press
P.O. Box 10
Yarmouth, Maine 04096
books@islandportpress.com
www.islandportpress.com

Text © 2015 by Carolyn Cory Scoppettone
Illustrations © 2015 by Priscilla Alpaugh Cotter

ISBN: 978-1-939017-68-0
Library of Congress Control Number: 2014959683

Production date: July 2015
Plant and location: Printed by We SP Corporation (Gyunggi-do, Korea)
Job / Batch #: 54193-0

For Sophia, Anna, and Nadia, and for Mom, always.
—CAROLYN SCOPPETTONE

For Lillian, who knew where the treasures were all along.
—PRISCILLA ALPAUGH

Down the woodland trail,
Mika leads the way.

Mika sees a sparkling stone.
"Will you hold this, Daddy?"

. . . a spiny spiral
pine cone.

"Hold this, too."

. . . a bumpy brittle
brown twig.

"And this!"

"Mika, you're a big girl,"
Daddy says.
"You can carry your own
treasures."

Mika stuffs the stone in her sleeve.
She puts the pine cone in her hood.
She waves the twig like a wand.

Oops!

Ouch!

Snap!

Sniff, sniff.

Daddy kisses away the tears.

They walk on. Mika hears . . .

the swissshhhing leaves

"Hold this."

"Hold this, too."

"And this."

the galumph galumph

croaking frog

"Mika, you're a big girl," Daddy says.
"But you can't carry all those treasures."

Mika tucks the leaves
behind her ear.

She balances the water
on her head.

She cradles
the frog in her fingers.

Bump!

Drip!

Jump!

Scowl!

Daddy hugs Mika. She wipes
her face on his shirt.

They walk on. Mika feels . . .

. . . the squishy mud.

"Hold this."

. . . the spongy umbrella mushroom.

"Hold this, too."

. . . the mossy
moist buggy log.
"And this."

"MIKA! You're a big girl," Daddy says,
"but not big enough
to pick up a rotten log."

Mika is busy by the tree.

"Daddy!" Mika calls.

"Come see my fairy house."

"Oh, my!" Daddy says.
"The fairies will be so happy."

"Daddy?" Mika says,
"I know I'm a big girl, but . . .

. . . Will you hold this?"

ABOUT THE AUTHOR

After working as a newspaper reporter in Los Angeles, Carolyn Cory Scoppettone moved to small-town New England to raise her children. Her new job as a freelance writer allowed time for walks in the woods. The children would race ahead, returning frequently with woodland treasures. Their sheer joy at exploring nature inspired Carolyn to write *Hold This!* In addition to picture books, Carolyn writes poetry, creative nonfiction, and middle grade novels. She lives in Montpelier, Vermont, with her husband Greg (a television director), their daughters, Sophia, Anna, and Nadia, plus two cats, one dog, and an energetic puppy.

Author photo by Michael T. Jermyn

ABOUT THE ARTIST

Priscilla Alpaugh earned her BFA in Painting and Illustration from UMass Amherst and studied for her MFA in Illustration at Syracuse University. Priscilla makes illustrations for the children's market and has also been known to paint murals and traffic control boxes, design logos and bookplates, and make digital animations. She works primarily in traditional mediums such as pencil, colored pencil, ink, and watercolor, but uses digital methods as required. A member of the Society of Children's Book Writers and Illustrators and the American Society of Bookplate Collectors and Designers, she lives in the greater Boston area with her family.

Artist photo by Fred Levy Photography